Place a photo of you & your Pop Pop here

For my Great—Uncle Clarence Pierce, who said I was his favorite
and taught me "I love you Black Child." — I.S.

In memory of my dad, Clint:
I can still smell your peach cobbler baking in the oven.
A little something for your sweet tooth. —C.A.J.

Clarence Pierce, Irene's Pop Pop

Second Edition Published 2014
Previously published in Hardcover as "My Pop Pop and Me"
ISBN: 0-316-73422-5

Paperback ISBN: 978-1-62395-586-1
eISBN: 978-1-62395-587-8
ePib ISBN: 978-1-62395-598-4
Published in the United States
by Xist Publishing
www.xistpublishing.com

xist Publishing

# Pop Pop and Me
## and a Recipe

written by **Irene Smalls**

illustrated by **Cathy Ann Johnson**

# Look, look
### my Pop Pop's a cook

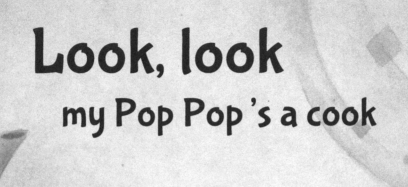

# Pat, Pat
### I love my chef's hat

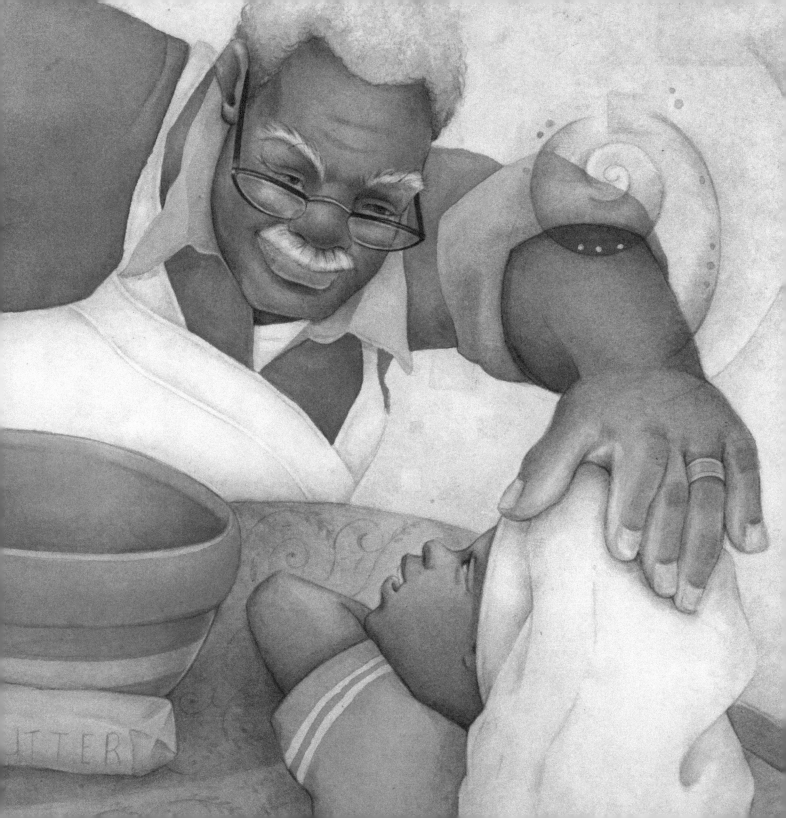

Scrub a dub dub

clean and rub

Bake, bake

my favorite cake

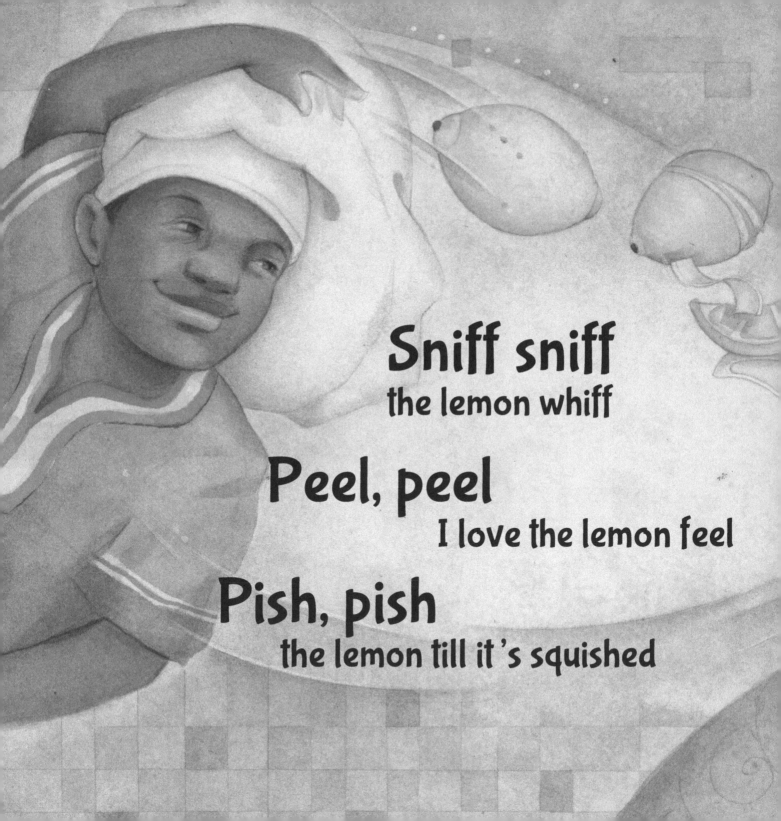

**Sniff sniff**
the lemon whiff

**Peel, peel**
I love the lemon feel

**Pish, pish**
the lemon till it's squished

**Pift, pift**
the sifter's swift

**Drip, drip**
milk into the batter bowl slips

**Mash, mash**

MOO MOO MILK

I love to smash

**Sizzle, sizzle**
the butter frizzles

**Twinkle, twinkle**
goes the salt I sprinkle

**Glop glop**
eggs into the batter plop

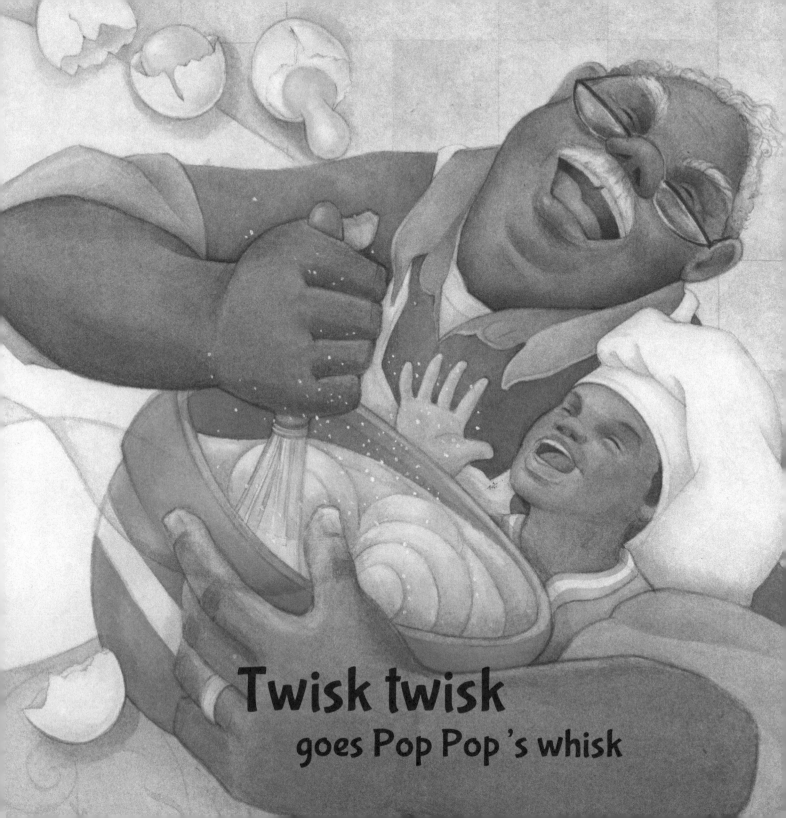

**Twisk twisk**
goes Pop Pop 's whisk

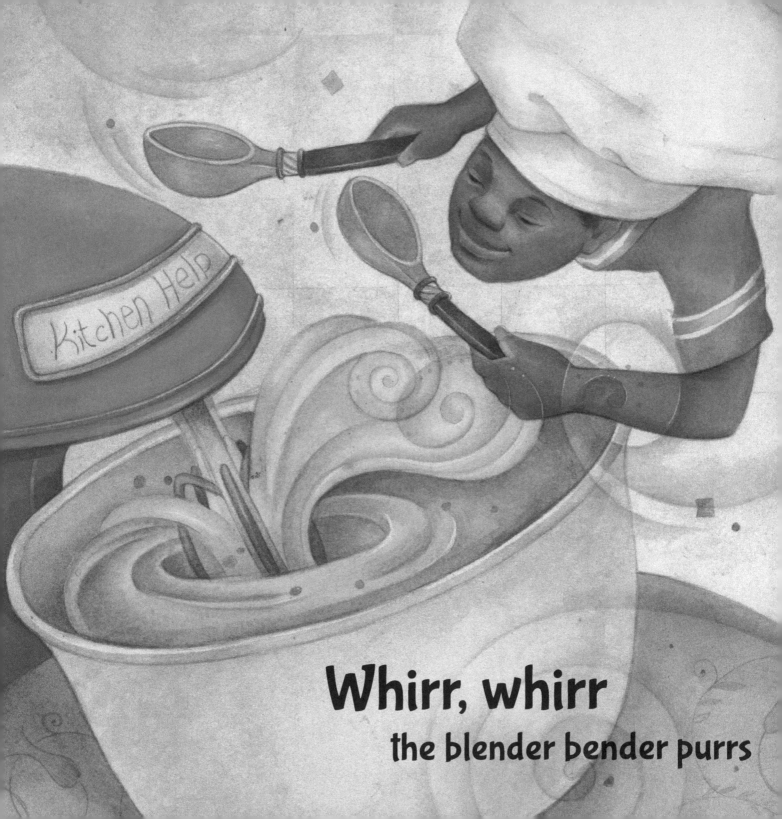

**Whirr, whirr**
the blender bender purrs

**Dip dip**
my finger to the tip

Pour pour
that's what batter's for

**Blat blat**
goes the batter I splat

**Swipe swipe**
the counter I wipe

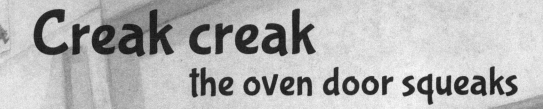

# Creak creak
## the oven door squeaks

# Make make
## the hissing cake bakes

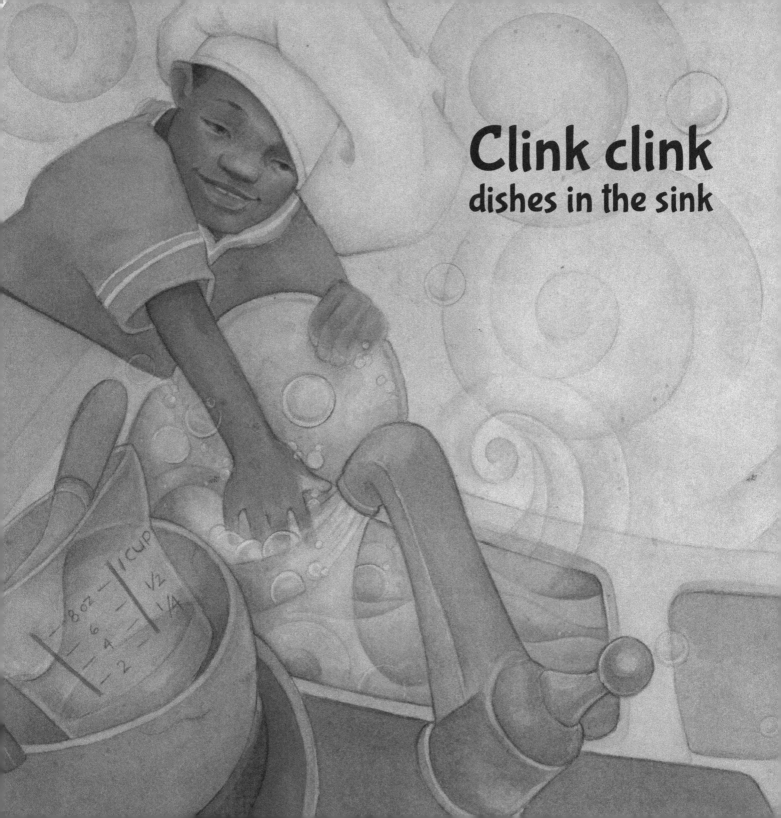

**Clink clink**
dishes in the sink

**Slosh slosh**
the dishes we wash

# Ding ding

the timer pings

Wheet wheet
the kettle tweets

Cool cool
that's the rule

# Slice slice
a big slice how nice!

# Yummy, yummy
lemon cake for the tummy

# Lemon Bar Cake Bake

**Utensils Needed:**
2 small bowls & 1 large bowl
1 flat 9 inch by 12 inch cake pan
Electric mixer or mix by hand 350 strokes
2 Large spoons
Measuring spoons & Measuring cup
Cake Tester - a clean tooth pick can be used as well
Wire rack or surface for cooling
Flour sifter
Preheated 350 degree oven
3 teaspoons cooking oil and flour to grease and flour cake pan

**Ingredients:**
4 Tablespoons lemon oil or lemon extract
2 tablespoons vanilla extract
2 cups cake flour
2 teaspoons baking powder
1/8 teaspoon salt (salt according to taste when doubling the recipe)
1 cup milk
1/2 cup lemon juice. Using fresh lemons juice two large lemons or three small lemons.
Take seeds out. Lemons skins can be zested to add a lemony look to your cake.
1 1/2 sticks softened or melted butter
2 cups sugar
3 beaten eggs

- Mix cake flour, baking powder, vanilla extract and salt together. Set aside
- Stir together, lemon juice, milk, lemon oil or extract, beaten eggs and butter in other small bowl.
- Mix all ingredients together in large bowl. Add sugar gradually to mixture beating it thoroughly.
- Coat cake pan with oil and flour. Shake loose any excess flour and discard
- Pour batter into cake pan(s). Bake at 350 degrees for 30 - 40 minutes. After 25 minutes stick a toothpick into the center. If it comes back clean the cake is done.
- Cool cake on a wire rack or cooling surface.

Note: To make the cake pictured on the cover, you will need to double the recipe. Bake in two 8 inch round pans, instead of one flat pan.

### Frosting Ingredients:
1 cup confectioner's or powdered sugar
2-6 tablespoons milk or other liquid
1 teaspoon lemon extract, more or less to taste

You need 3-4 cups of frosting for the layer cake shown on the cover.
- For the layer cake add 2 teaspoons finely grated lemon rind as a topping
- Measure the sugar into a bowl. Add 2 tablespoons of milk and the extract.
- Stir until it forms a thick, creamy paste.

Frosting will keep refrigerated in a sealed container for up to a week.

CPSIA information can be obtained
at www.ICGtesting.com
Printed in the USA
LVHW072341150819
627873LV00019B/68/P